I WANT CAKE!

Written by:
Danielle A Renning

Tellwell Talent
www.tellwell.ca

ISBN
978-0-2288-5048-9 (Hardcover)
978-0-2288-5047-2 (Paperback)

Dedicated with love to:

Benjamin, Emily and Olivia

We can achieve and receive all we desire,
never give up and never retire,
your dreams and wishes, to yourselves stay true,
anything can happen, always believe in
YOU

With all my love forever and always:

Auntie

xox

"I want cake! I want cake! I want cake!" cried Nat and Jake.

"First, before we have some cake, let's
take some time for us to bake."

"BAKE A CAKE!? WE WANT IT NOW! We don't
have time; we don't know how!"

"We have the time; you will learn how. There
will be cake; just not right now."

"I will learn, and I will wait. I am ready to participate!"

"We will make our cake once lunch is done. I will need help gathering the ingredients, this will be fun."

"I don't care; I don't want to wait. I don't want to learn how to bake a cake!"

Nat decided to sit and pout. She plopped herself upon the couch. She watched the two as they started to make what Nana promised would be... an unforgettable chocolate cake.

Nat, now stressed, arms crossed on her chest, asked, "WHY CAN'T WE BUY THE CAKE AND SKIP THIS BIG MESS!?"

"It's not just cake we're making, dear. Come back
to the kitchen and watch from in here."

Nat returned to the kitchen, fuming inside; she
kept on wishing Nana would just go drive!

Nat sat on the chair with a glare on her face,
but in a few moments, her glare did erase.

The joy and the mess and all the laughter she saw made
her look over at the corner of Nana's messy kitchen wall.
On this wall Nana had wrote herself a personal little note:

Nat after seeing the note on the wall, now knew
Nana's reason to bake after all. Nana wants to teach
us a fun new way to have what we want but not
right away. For us to learn the value of patience and
quality time to learn new skills to grow our mind.

"Okay, dear Jake, it's time to pour. Let's
not spill this batter on the floor."

Jake poured the cake batter: it splatted, it sprayed. As
the dish fell and broke, he didn't know what to say.

And once all the noise came to a stop, they broke
out in laughter from being covered in slop!

"You dropped the dish; you've spilled all the batter! The kitchen's a mess and I am covered in splatter! All the hard work to now have no cake, why couldn't you be more careful Jake!?"

"You see, my dear Nat, this is not only about cake but also the laughter and learning when we try to bake. You can demand the cake, ingredients too, but what matters the most is the work that you do. The things that we want may not come as we wish, just like this cake and my broken dish. Now that we have no more batter for cake, would you like to try again? This time with me, you, and Jake?"

All three cleaned the kitchen and they went right back at'er, mixing a batch of fresh chocolate cake batter.

They laughed and told stories, sprayed and splatted some
more. Nana did not care how much got on the floor.

Once all the batter was mixed and looked oh so sweet,
Jake poured it again — mostly onto their feet.

"Careful, Jake, or you'll do it once more: you'll spill all the batter it will fall to the floor!" Nat growing impatient and hungry for cake, not wanting a repeat of Jake's messy mistake.

"Nat, my dearest, that is okay. No matter what we will have cake today. It may be messy and take us a few tries, but learning together is the real prize."

While the three of them waited for the cake to complete, they cleaned up the kitchen, making it tidy and neat. As Nat began to smell the cake, becoming impatient, she did not want to wait.

"I hate cleaning. I don't want to wait. I just want to eat a piece of this cake!"

"Oh, my dearest Nat and Jake, we want, we want, we want all the time. You can demand the cake, yes this is true, but what matters most is the work that you do. Through the work and the time, it takes to make cake, you will learn from every single mistake. To practice, have fun, and laugh along the way is what makes this cake special for us today. You said you want cake and it's cake you will have. It's patience you're learning, so please don't be mad."

"BING BING!" sang the oven to let them all know
the cake was ready — and oh boy did it grow!

Nana took the warm cake out of the oven to cool. With
the smell of fresh cake, it was hard not to drool!

When the cake, cooled and sliced, was placed on the table,
the three tired bakers were now finally able to taste this
very special treat. They had learned something new, and that
was pretty neat! All the smiles and cake that they did eat
were as sweet as the memories they would now get to keep.

Always have patience, and always be kind and never give up when having a hard time.

Written by:

Danielle A Renning

CPSIA information can be obtained
at www.ICGtesting.com
Printed in the USA
BVHW020102201021
619351BV00003B/10